**Dear Parents and Teac**

D0816393

In an easy-reader format, **My Readers** introduce classic stories to children who are learning to read. Favorite characters and time-tested tales are the basis for **My Readers**, which are available in three levels:

1   **Level One** is for the emergent reader and features repetitive language and word clues in the illustrations.

2   **Level Two** is for more advanced readers who still need support saying and understanding some words. Stories are longer with word clues in the illustrations.

3   **Level Three** is for independent, fluent readers who enjoy working out occasional unfamiliar words. The stories are longer and divided into chapters.

Encourage children to select books based on interests, not reading levels. Read aloud with children, showing them how to use the illustrations for clues. With adult guidance and rereading, children will eventually read the desired book on their own.

Here are some ways you might want to use this book with children:

- Talk about the title and the cover illustrations. Encourage the child to use these to predict what the story is about.
- Discuss the interior illustrations and try to piece together a story based on the pictures. Does the child want to change or adjust his first prediction?
- After children reread a story, suggest they retell or act out a favorite part.

My Readers will not only help children become readers, they will serve as an introduction to some of the finest classic children's books available today.

—LAURA ROBB
Educator and Reading Consultant

For activities and reading tips, visit myreadersonline.com.

For Mabel Grace
—J. G.

For my family
—N. R.

SQUARE
FISH

An Imprint of Macmillan Children's Publishing Group

ROTTEN RALPH HELPS OUT. Text copyright © 2001 by Jack Gantos.
Pictures copyright © 2001 by Nicole Rubel. All rights reserved.
Printed in China by Toppan Leefung, Dongguan City, Guangdong Province.
For information, address Square Fish, 175 Fifth Avenue, New York, NY 10010.

Library of Congress Cataloging-in-Publication Data
Gantos, Jack.
Rotten Ralph helps out / Jack Gantos and Nicole Rubel.
p.   cm.
Summary: Sarah's cat Rotten Ralph tries to help her create a school project based
on ancient Egypt, but he is more of a hindrance than a help.
[1. Cats—Fiction. 2. Egypt—Civilization—To 322 B.C.—Fiction. 3. Homework—Fiction.
4. Schools—Fiction.] I. Rubel, Nicole. II. Title.

PZ7.G15334 Roh 2001   [E]—dc21   00-39405

ISBN 978-0-312-64172-6 (hardcover)
1 3 5 7 9 10 8 6 4 2

ISBN 978-0-312-67281-2 (paperback)
1 3 5 7 9 10 8 6 4 2

Book design by Patrick Collins/Véronique Lefèvre Sweet

Square Fish logo designed by Filomena Tuosto

The character of Rotten Ralph was originally created by Jack Gantos and Nicole Rubel.

Originally published: Farrar Straus Giroux, 2001
First My Readers Edition: 2012

myreadersonline.com
mackids.com

This is a Level 3 book

AR: 3.0 / LEXILE: 430L

R⦿tten Ralph
Helps Out

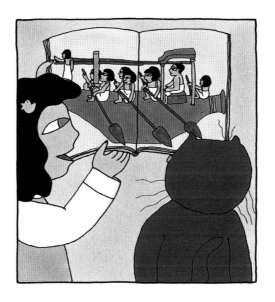

written by **Jack Gantos**

illustrated by **Nicole Rubel**

SQUARE
FISH

Macmillan Children's Publishing Group
New York

Contents

Walk Like an Egyptian

One morning, Sarah was walking
like an Egyptian.
She had been learning
all about the ancient Egyptians
for a big school project.
"Don't you think
I look like Cleopatra,
queen of the Nile?"
she asked Rotten Ralph
when he woke up.

Ralph was too hungry to care
about Cleopatra or the Egyptians.
He walked into the kitchen
and smelled pancakes.
"Do you know where pancakes
come from?" Sarah asked.
The store, Ralph said to himself.
"Ancient Egypt," Sarah said.
"The Egyptians made
the very first pancakes."
That's funny, Ralph thought.
They don't taste old and moldy.
He burped loudly.

"Ralph!" scolded Sarah.
"Mind your manners!
Thanks to the Egyptians,
you are not a wild animal."

Sarah informed Ralph that the Egyptians
were the first people to have cats for pets.
If it were up to me, Ralph thought,
it would be the other way around.

Sarah was going to the library
to read more about Egypt
for her school project.
"Ralph, I'm sure you can help me
think of something great to build,"
she said. "After all,
the ancient Egyptians
believed cats were very wise
and had special powers."
How about building
a special litter box for *your* wise cat?
Ralph suggested.

Sarah filled her red wagon

with books to return to the library.

She climbed in and asked Ralph

to pull the wagon down the sidewalk.

"I bet you didn't know the Egyptians loved to ride in chariots," said Sarah. I bet they didn't pull the chariots themselves, Ralph groaned.

Read Like an Egyptian

When they arrived at the library,

Sarah told Ralph

that the ancient Egyptians

had libraries, too.

"People had to be quiet then,"

she whispered,

"and they have to be quiet now."

It's as *quiet* as a tomb in here,

Ralph thought.

"Ralph," said Sarah,

"I want you to sit down

and read this book on the pyramids.

Maybe building a pyramid

would be a good school project."

Sarah went to find

a book about Cleopatra.

Reading about the pyramids

gave Ralph big ideas.

He built a giant pyramid out of books.

"Ralph!" cried Sarah.

"Books are not building blocks!"

Ralph jumped off,

and the pyramid crashed to the floor.

"Control yourself!" said the librarian.

"Now sit down and read,"
Sarah ordered. "You will like
this book about mummies."
But Ralph's fur stood on end
when he saw what Egyptians did to cats.

He crawled to the top of a bookshelf.

Sarah came running over.

"Ralph! Don't be a scaredy-cat.

Come down here and behave."

She gave Ralph another book.

"The Egyptians invented

their own special kind of writing,"

she said. "They used pictures

instead of letters."

She went to read more

about how Cleopatra was

the most powerful woman in Egypt.

She had a huge army,

and a palace filled with adoring cats.

The librarian caught Ralph

writing all over the walls.

She marched him over to Sarah.

"I'm sorry," she said,

"but you and your naughty cat

will have to leave."

Sarah was embarrassed.

She wondered

if Cleopatra had ever been

this angry with

one of her cats.

Shake Like an Egyptian

"Every time I want to do

something fun, you spoil it,"

said Sarah when they returned home.

"I wish you would learn how to help."

Ralph felt rotten.

He was ready to help.

He stuck out his paw.

"Okay, let's shake on it,"

said Sarah.

"After all, the Egyptians

invented the handshake."

"Maybe we should build
a model of an Egyptian boat?"
Sarah suggested.
Rotten Ralph loved the idea
and got busy.

30

But he let the tub overflow

and began to float down the hallway.

"Ralph," cried Sarah,

"please don't flood the house!"

Sarah decided that building
a desert oasis might be better.
Ralph filled his wheelbarrow
with sand and made a pile
in the living room.

He spread it around with a shovel.

He planted palm trees.

But Ralph's helping

only upset Sarah.

He was making an Egyptian mess.

Then Ralph remembered

his bug collection.

Sarah had said

the Egyptians loved beetles.

He ran to show his bugs to Sarah.

But he tripped over a palm tree.

Bugs landed

all over Sarah's dress.

It was so disgusting

she moaned out loud.

"I can't take your helping anymore!"

she said.

"Ralph, you've been working so hard, why don't you go to bed early?"

Ralph yawned.

Helping does make me tired, he thought.

While Sarah watched Ralph sleep, she felt bad for getting upset.

Suddenly, she had a great idea.

Cleopatra loved cats just as I do, she thought. I should build a model of Cleopatra and her favorite cat.

She got some wire

and twisted it into a shape.

Then she made some papier-mâché

and smoothed it over the wire.

Perfect! she thought.

I will paint it in the morning.

And she went to bed happy.

Look Like an Egyptian

Ralph woke up

and saw what Sarah had made.

That doesn't look very special,

he thought.

Sarah still needs my help.

But when Sarah saw what Ralph had done,

she was not happy.

"Ralph!" she cried.

"You've ruined my statue of Cleopatra.

Now I have nothing for my project.

My teacher is going to be

very disappointed."

Ralph hung his head.

He had let Sarah down again.

"What am I going to do?"

said Sarah.

She went to her room to think.

Ralph did some thinking, too.

Sarah and the Egyptians are right,

he thought.

Cats are very wise,

and we do have special powers.

Ralph got busy all over again.

When Sarah saw what he was up to,

 she was thrilled.

"Why didn't I think of this myself?"

she said.

Ralph had dressed up

as the Sphinx,

the most famous Egyptian cat

of all time.

Sarah's teacher was impressed.

Her school friends were impressed.

Of course,

Ralph was impressed with himself.

Sarah's classmates had

good projects, too.

One showed how the Egyptians

invented checkers.

One wore a big red fez.

One even charmed a garden snake

with an Egyptian flute.

Sarah's teacher praised all their work.

On the way home, Sarah wheeled Ralph

to the candy shop for a treat.

I love candy, Ralph thought.

"I know you do," Sarah said.

"After all, the ancient Egyptians

were wise enough to invent candy.

And the Sphinx is the wisest cat of all."